The Passionate Pursuit: A Tale of Forbidden Love and Unbridled Desire

IVY BLAIR

Published by RWG Publishing, 2023.

THE PASSIONATE PURSUIT: A TALE OF FORBIDDEN LOVE AND UNBRIDLED DESIRE

First edition. May 3, 2023.

Written by IVY BLAIR.

Also by IVY BLAIR

Breathless Desire: A Tale of Passion and Obsession
The Perfect Match: A Love Story Written in the Stars
The Passionate Pursuit: A Tale of Forbidden Love and Unbridled
Desire

Table of Contents

Chapter 1: The First Glance - A Moment of Intense Connection

The moment their gazes connected, a spark was immediately set off between them. She stood out like a bright light in the darkness despite the fact that the room was full of people from different backgrounds and walks of life. He was attracted to her in the same way that a moth is drawn to a flame. She was radiant, and her smile could brighten even the darkest of nights; as a result, he found himself completely captivated by her.

Even though she was across the room having a conversation with a group of her friends, he was unable to take his eyes off of her. It was as if everything else in the world had vanished, and she was the only thing left. He couldn't place his finger on what it was, but he knew it was a pull toward her, like a magnetic attraction. Because he could feel his heart beating faster, he was aware that he needed to speak to her.

He made his way across the room, navigating his way through the crowd while keeping his gaze fixed on her the entire time. As he got closer, he could feel his anxiety rising to the surface and taking over his body. What thoughts would he have? What if she didn't have any interest in it? He pushed those thoughts out of his mind and took a moment to steady himself by taking a deep breath.

After he had finally reached her, she turned around to face him, and the two of them looked at each other with their eyes locked once more. He was left unable to catch his breath after feeling a jolt run through his body, which was followed by a surge of electricity. It was unlike anything he had ever encountered or felt in the past.

"Hi," he finally managed to utter, his voice barely rising above a whisper.

"Hello," she said in response, her smile remaining fixed on her face the entire time.

After they started talking to each other, it seemed as though they had known each other for many years. They laughed together and shared stories for what seemed like hours, but he had no idea how much time had passed. Even though he didn't want the night to end, they had no choice but to part ways at some point.

As he walked away, he was aware that he had just been a part of a very memorable experience. He was at a loss for words, but he had the distinct impression that he had just made contact with his true love. He was aware that he needed to visit her once more.

Something had been sparked in him at the first glance, something that he simply could not ignore. He was hooked.

Chapter 2: Unspoken Desires - The Thrill of the Forbidden

E ven though it had been several weeks since their initial encounter, he was unable to stop thinking about her. They had begun texting and calling one another after exchanging phone numbers, but it was never enough between the two of them. He was looking for more. He longed to be in her presence once more and experience the same jolt of excitement that he had felt the first time they had spoken.

However, there was a catch in the scenario. She had an official spouse.

He was aware that he should avoid her and that it was inappropriate for him to pursue her, but he was powerless to change the way that he felt. He was attracted to her in the same way that a moth would be drawn to a flame, and the more they conversed, the clearer it became that she felt the same way about him.

They would talk for hours, sharing their fears and insecurities as well as their hopes and dreams with one another. They shared a bond that he had never experienced with anyone else, and he was aware that he was powerless to deny its existence.

However, the more he spoke to her, the more guilty he felt about what had happened. He was well aware that what they were doing was immoral and that he was putting not only his own but also her potential for happiness in jeopardy by participating in it. He didn't want to be the one who caused anyone any suffering or emotional anguish.

Despite this, it was impossible to deny the urge any longer. He yearned to be in her presence, to experience the sensation of her touch, and to cradle her in his arms. The fact that one could not fulfill their wish made the experience all the more exciting.

He was aware that he needed to exercise caution and that they needed to maintain the confidentiality of their gatherings. They would get together in secret, far from prying eyes, and those were the times when they experienced the most vibrant levels of life.

The excitement of doing something that was against the rules was addicting. They would steal kisses from one another and look at each other with knowing looks, and it was as if there were no one else in the world but the two of them. They were aware that it was a risky game, but neither of them wanted it to end even though it was getting increasingly dangerous.

But despite their best efforts to keep their emotions in check, they were aware that things were quickly getting out of hand for them. They were already in over their heads, and they had no idea how to get out of it.

He was aware that he needed to make a choice. Either he had to get out of there, put an end to things before it was too late, or he had to face his fears and go all in on what he was doing. He couldn't stand the idea of parting ways with her, but at the same time, he didn't want to be the one to make her unhappy.

The fact that they did not express their desires to one another was driving a wedge between them. He was aware of his desires, but he was uncertain about his capacity to deal with the outcomes of those desires.

He was addicted to the rush that came from doing something that was against the rules, and he just couldn't stop. But he was also aware that it had the potential to ruin everything that he treasured. It was a risky game, but he wasn't entirely confident that he could get out of it alive.

Chapter 3: The Dance of Seduction - A Dangerous Game Begins

Their once-warm relationship had become fraught with peril. What had begun as harmless teasing had developed into a full-blown affair, and he was well aware that they were both putting themselves in danger by continuing the relationship.

The dance of seduction had begun, and now he was completely captivated by its enchantment. He was well aware that he was putting everything on the line, but he was powerless to stop the way he felt. She was to him what a drug would be to another person, and he needed his fix.

They would get together in the shadows, constantly looking over their shoulders for fear of being discovered. But the presence of risk only served to heighten the sense of adventure. It was as if they were living in their own private enclave, oblivious to the outside world and the norms it imposed.

They were competing against one another, but coming out on top in the game that was the dance of seduction. They would tease one another and touch each other in ways that would make their hearts race, and he knew that they were both living in the moment even as he watched them.

But he was also aware that it couldn't continue on like this forever. They would be apprehended at some point, and when they were, the repercussions would be severe. He didn't want to be the one to cause her discomfort, but he also couldn't abandon her at this point.

The risky game that they were playing was similar to walking a tightrope, and he wasn't sure if he could maintain his equilibrium throughout it. The seduction was all-consuming, and he was aware that it had the potential to cause him to lose everything that he treasured in his life.

Knowing that he had betrayed not only her but also himself, he was unable to stop himself from experiencing feelings of guilt. He had never considered the possibility that he might be the type of person who would have an affair, but here he was, knee-deep in a relationship with someone else.

He was well aware that the dance of seduction was a risky game and that he was putting himself in harm's way. However, he was unable to restrain himself in any way. The attraction he felt for her was insurmountable, and he was well aware that he had no choice but to carry on with the game.

Even though he had no idea what the future held, he was certain that he would never stop being attracted to her. The dance of seduction had begun, and he was already too far along to back out of it at this point.

Chapter 4: Secrets and Lies - The High Price of Forbidden Love

They had to keep more secrets and lies a secret the longer they were forced to spend time together. They were leading two separate lives, and it was beginning to show signs of strain on both of them.

He was unable to discuss the affair with anyone, not even those closest to him in his life. He was always worried that someone would find out the truth and ruin everything he had spent so much time and effort achieving. On the other hand, he was unable to refrain from looking at her.

The heavy burden of paying the high price of illicit love had become intolerable. He was consistently dishonest and attempted to cover his tracks, but he was well aware that it was only a matter of time before everything he had built would come tumbling down.

She was in the same position as you are, constantly needing to devise explanations for why she was out late or why she had to leave early. She was in the same boat as you. The lies were having a negative impact, and he was aware that both of them were beginning to feel guilty.

But despite his best efforts, he was unable to put an end to it. He had fallen hopelessly in love with her, and the prospect of having to live without her was intolerable to him. He was willing to put up with the deceit and deception even though it was a high price to pay for the woman he loved.

He was well aware that what they were doing was improper and that they were putting everything that they had toiled so diligently to achieve in jeopardy. But the love that they had for one another made it all worthwhile. He was unable to picture his life without her presence in it.

It was getting more and more challenging to conceal the lies and the secrets, and he was well aware that they would eventually be discovered. He wasn't sure if he could keep paying the price of forbidden love because it was such a high cost to him.

It was up to him to make a choice. Either he had to put an end to the affair and admit what he had been doing, or he had to face the consequences and carry on. He was aware of the outcomes of both, but he was unable to determine which was more detrimental.

The high cost of forbidden love was taking its toll on him, and he wasn't sure how much longer he could continue to keep it up. He didn't know how long he could keep it up. On the other hand, he was conscious of the fact that he was unable to abandon her. He wasn't sure if he could survive without the love that they had for one another because it was so powerful.

He was becoming increasingly burdened by the lies and secrets, and he realized that he could not continue to live his life in this manner indefinitely. It was up to him to make a decision, but he wasn't sure if he possessed the mental fortitude to pick the best option.

Chapter 5: The First Kiss - A Taste of What's to Come

It was a pleasant evening in the middle of summer, and they were both sitting in his car, conversing and laughing as they regularly did. But things were different this time. He was able to sense the tension that existed between them, as well as the electricity that seemed to be present whenever they were in the same room together.

Before he knew it, he was attempting to kiss her and he had no idea what had possessed him to act in such a manner. And she did not attempt to escape.

A foretaste of what was to come, the first kiss was like a jolt of electricity and a taste of what was to come. He had never experienced anything even remotely similar to it before, and he was aware that this was just the beginning of things to come.

They kissed each other as if there was no tomorrow, their ardor and hunger for one another growing stronger with every passing second. It was as if they had both been lacking in affection for a very long time, and now they were at last getting their fill.

The foretaste of what was to come thrilled him, and he couldn't wait to experience the rest of it. He desired to examine every part of her, to feel her weight against his, and to discover whether or not this was a dream or a reality.

But despite the fact that he desperately wanted to get lost in the experience, he was well aware that they needed to exercise caution. They had to keep their affair a secret from everyone, which required them to maintain some physical distance from one another when they were in public together.

The first time they kissed marked a turning point in their relationship, and he knew then that things would never be the same between them again. They had crossed a threshold, and there was no going back now that they had done so.

On the other hand, he was aware of the fact that he had no desire to return. He knew that he was addicted to her because the flavor of what was to come was too sweet and he was dependent on her.

The first kiss had been the trigger that started everything, and he was well aware that there was no turning back now. He had gotten a small taste of what was to come, and he knew that in order to be with her, he would do anything that was necessary. He was powerless to resist.

It was a moment that he would never forget, a taste of what was to come, and he was more than willing to pay the high price of forbidden love to experience it again and again. The first kiss was a moment that he would never forget.

Chapter 6: The Lure of the Unknown - Risking it All

The allure of the unknowable was something that had a powerful pull on him throughout his life. He had never been someone who shied away from taking chances and was never afraid to go after what he wanted. And with her, the mystery of the unknowable held even more appeal.

He was aware that what they were doing was dangerous, and that by engaging in it, not only were they jeopardizing their own happiness but also the happiness of those around them. On the other hand, it was impossible to resist the allure of the unknowable.

He had no idea how things would turn out, but he was certain that he couldn't just walk away from this situation. It was impossible to deny the intensity of the attraction, and the very idea of carrying on without her was intolerable.

He was willing to put himself in potentially dangerous situations in order to play the game of the unknown. He felt attracted to her in the same way that a moth is drawn to a flame, and he was aware that he would go to any lengths to be with her.

The excitement of venturing into the unknown was all-consuming for him, and he found himself constantly thinking about her. When they were in public together, he couldn't help but steal a look at her, which set his heart pounding with excitement.

He was aware that he was putting everything on the line, but he also was aware that the reward was well worth the risk. The idea of being with her and having her by his side was so alluring that he could not resist giving in to it.

Even though he had no idea where the road would take them, he was willing to take the chance nonetheless. He was prepared to put everything on the line in order to have the opportunity to be with her.

He was aware that he was putting everything on the line, but he couldn't resist the allure of venturing into the unknown. On the other hand, he was well aware of the fact that he would perish in her absence.

He was caught up in the enchantment of the unknown, which turned out to be an exciting game. Even though he had no idea how things would turn out, he was determined to keep playing even if it meant resorting to any means necessary.

He was unable to ignore the call of the unknown, despite the fact that he was well aware that he was putting everything on the line. But he knew that as long as she was by his side, he could conquer any challenge.

He was willing to put himself in potentially dangerous situations in order to play the game of the unknown. He was putting everything on the line, but he knew it would be well worth it if it meant he could spend more time with her.

Chapter 7: The Heat of the Moment - Passion Ignites

The intensity of the situation consumed me completely. They were by themselves, their bodies pressed against each other, and he could feel the passion rising within him despite the fact that they were alone.

He had no idea how it had happened, but suddenly he found himself completely absorbed in the activity at hand and in her. Their bodies moved in harmony, their lust for one another stoking the fires of their passion.

He had never been in a situation where the pressure was quite as intense as it was right then. It was as if they were both in a trance, lost in the intensity of the desire and passion that they had in common.

They moved as one, their hands exploring every inch of each other as they went. The intensity of the situation was intoxicating, and he found that he was unable to focus on anything else while it was happening.

He was well aware that what they were doing was inappropriate and that they were putting their entire future in jeopardy. When it came down to it, none of that was relevant in the heat of the moment. The enthusiasm that they both possessed was the only thing that counted.

The intensity of the situation was addictive, and he just couldn't get enough of it. He desired to be in her presence, to sense her touch, and to have confirmation that what they shared was genuine.

He was unsure of how everything would play out, but he was certain that he did not want it to come to an end. Because the passion they shared was too intense, he knew that he would do anything to keep it going even if it meant sacrificing himself.

The intensity of the moment, which was a moment of unadulterated ardor and yearning, was something that he would never forget. It was an instant that would haunt him for the rest of his life, serving as a constant reminder of the illicit love that they had for one another.

He was aware that the intensity of the situation was potentially harmful and that it had the potential to compromise everything they held most dear. But he was also aware that he was unable to flee the scene. The passion that they shared was insurmountable, and he was prepared to put everything on the line for it.

The intensity of the situation was comparable to a fire that could not be put out at any time. It burned inside of him, stoking the fire of his desire for her, and he was well aware that he was willing to do anything to keep it going as long as possible.

The fire of passion that was stoked by the intensity of the situation was an experience that he would never let go of. It served as a constant reminder of the illicit love that the two of them had for one another, and he was prepared to do anything to protect their relationship.

Chapter 8: The Morning After - Guilt and Regret

The following morning was always the most difficult. He felt guilty and ashamed of what they had done when he woke up next to her the next morning.

He was well aware of the fact that what they were doing was improper and that they were putting everything they had worked for in jeopardy. But in the heat of the moment, all of that seemed to melt away and become irrelevant.

The feelings of guilt and regret that he was experiencing were overwhelming. When he turned around to face her, he couldn't bring himself to look her in the eye because of what they had done.

He desired to put an end to the affair and be truthful about what had been going on. On the other hand, he was conscious of the fact that he was unable to abandon her. The very idea of being without her was too painful to bear.

The next morning was a harsh reminder of the consequences of the actions that they had taken the night before. He was well aware that they were putting everything on the line and that their affair had the potential to undo all of their hard work.

The feelings of guilt and regret that he had were like a burden that was constantly pressing down on his shoulders. He was aware that he needed to take action of some kind in order to make up for what they had done.

But he was also aware that he couldn't complete the task by himself. He required her presence at his side in order to jointly deal with the repercussions of their actions.

The following morning served as a rude awakening and a sobering reminder of the peril they had put themselves in. He was aware that he needed to make a choice, and he could either put an end to the affair and admit the truth, or he could take the risk and continue on.

The feelings of guilt and regret were wearing him down to the point where he realized he couldn't go on living this way for much longer. It was up to him to make a decision, but he wasn't sure if he possessed the mental fortitude to pick the best option.

The morning after was a defining moment for him, a time when he was forced to confront the results of his actions and face the truth about what he had done. He was aware that he needed to make amends in order to attempt to put things back on the right track.

He felt as though he was being followed by a shadow of guilt and regret wherever he went. He had no idea how to get away from it or how to put things back in order.

The next morning was a harsh reminder of the price they were paying for their forbidden love, and it was a reminder that they had to pay. Although the feelings of guilt and regret were a heavy burden on him, he was aware that he was unable to abandon her.

Chapter 9: The Forbidden Tryst - A Moment of Pure Ecstasy

They had been preparing for this event for several weeks, and now it was finally going to take place. They both yearned for the illicit encounter, but they were well aware of the dangers involved in doing so. They had located a place that was hidden from prying eyes, and once there, they were left to their own devices. The timing was impeccable, and he could feel the thrill of anticipation racing through his veins. They began slowly, their touches being light and gentle from the beginning. However, as the intensity of their feelings increased, their movements became more hurried and desperate. It was a moment of pure ecstasy for him, and he knew that he would never forget the forbidden tryst they shared together. They moved as one, their bodies moving in perfect harmony with one another, and the desire they had for one another grew stronger with each passing moment. When he felt her skin against his, he realized that everything he was experiencing was actually happening. He wished that the moment could have continued on indefinitely because it was so wonderful. The illicit tryst was a moment of pure ecstasy for him, a moment when he felt more alive than he ever had before. He desired to become completely immersed in the experience at hand, to forget about everything else and concentrate solely on her company. But he was aware that it couldn't continue on like this forever.

They would eventually have to return to their lives and be forced to deal with the repercussions of the decisions they made. A reminder of the high cost they were paying for their forbidden love was the tryst that they were not allowed to have. But in this very instant, he didn't give a damn about it. The only thing that mattered to him was the passion that he shared with her. It was the kind of moment that could only be described as pure ecstasy. He was well aware that he would never forget it, and that it would serve as a constant reminder of the illicit love that the two of them shared for one another. The illicit tryst was a moment of unparalleled pleasure for him, a moment in which he felt more alive than ever before. He wanted to cling to the sensation and ensure that he would never lose it. However, as the moment came to an end, he was aware that he would have to deal with the repercussions that were caused by his actions. The illicit tryst served as a reminder that their love was risky and that it had the potential to destroy everything that was important to them. It was the kind of moment that could only be described as pure ecstasy. However, he was aware that he needed to be cautious in order to maintain the privacy of their affair and safeguard the relationships they shared with the people they cared about. The forbidden tryst was a moment in his life that he would never forget, a moment filled with unbridled desire and passion. It was a constant reminder of the illicit love that they had for one another and the terrible price that they had to pay for it.

Chapter 10: The Power of Words - Declarations of Love

They had been seeing each other for a number of months, and it was about time that they moved their relationship to the next level. He was conscious of the fact that he loved her, and he desired for her to be aware of this.

Even though he had never been particularly gifted with language, he was aware that he needed to find a way to communicate the emotions he was experiencing. He desired to express to her how significant she was in his life and how deeply he loved her.

He had never before really grasped the concept of the power of words, but now he realized that communicating his emotions through language was the only option available to him.

He expressed his feelings for her in a letter that he had written for her. He expressed to her his utmost affection for her, how much she meant to him, and how he could not conceive of living his life without her by his side.

He was aware that it was a gamble and that there was a possibility that she would not feel the same way. But he had to seize the opportunity to tell her how he truly felt about her.

He had a fundamental misunderstanding of the power that words possess. The things that he had written had an impact on her feelings, and she had responded to his feelings in kind.

Everything had been turned upside down by the passionate declarations of love. They were no longer just two individuals having an affair; rather, they had fallen in love with one another.

The power of words had allowed a door to be opened, and he was aware that once it had been opened, there was no turning back. He had confessed his love for her, and she had shown that she felt the same way. They were now in this situation together, whether it turned out well or not.

They had grown closer to one another as a result of the declarations of love, and he had no doubt that their love was genuine. It wasn't just a one-night stand; there was more to it than that.

They had been set on a new course by the power of words, a course that led to love and commitment. He was well aware that it wouldn't be simple, especially considering that they were still required to conceal their affair, but he was ready to do whatever it took to be with her.

He had found a glimmer of hope in the midst of the darkness that was their forbidden love thanks to the declarations of love that she had given him. He was aware that they were putting themselves in harm's way and that their love was risky, but he was prepared to deal with the repercussions of their actions.

Everything had been turned upside down as a result of the power of words, and he was certain that he would never, ever forget this moment. It was a moment of unadulterated love and dedication, a moment that would remain ingrained in his memory for the rest of his life.

The confessions of love marked a turning point in their relationship, a moment in which he realized that he would give up everything to be with her. They had grown closer to one another through the power of words, and he knew that their love was something that was worth fighting for.

Chapter 11: The Fear of Discovery - Keeping the Secret

The worry that he would be found out was something that was constantly present in the back of his mind. He was well aware of the fact that what they were doing was improper and that they were putting everything they had worked for in jeopardy.

Because they wanted to keep their affair a secret, they needed to be very careful. They couldn't risk anyone finding out about it because it would jeopardize everything that was important to them.

The worry that someone would find out about him was one of the things that weighed heavily on him. He was unsure how much longer they would be able to maintain the pretense, or how much longer they would be able to conceal their love for one another.

He was aware of the necessity for them to watch their step at all times and exercise extreme caution. They could not risk anyone becoming suspicious, or else everything would be ruined.

The worry about being found out was like a shadow that accompanied him wherever he went. No matter how hard he tried to get away from it, he was unable to do so.

They were required to be cautious in their actions because they could not be sure that no one was watching them. They were unable to take any chances of being discovered because it would put an end to everything.

They had to live in constant terror of being caught, which served as a constant reminder of the high cost of their illicit relationship. No matter how difficult it was for them, they had to keep the secret to themselves.

He was well aware that they were putting their lives in jeopardy and that their love was risky. On the other hand, he was conscious of the fact that he was unable to abandon her. The very idea of being without her was too painful to bear.

He lived in constant dread of being found out, and it was one of the things that kept him on edge. It was imperative that he watch his step at all times and maintain a state of heightened vigilance.

He was aware that they were putting themselves in harm's way and that their love was perilous. On the other hand, he was well aware of the fact that he would perish in her absence. He was willing to pay the price for her, despite the fact that the constant worry that they would be found out was a constant reminder of the price they were paying.

He felt as though he had a weight on his shoulders from the worry that someone would find out, but he was aware that he couldn't run away. Their love was unbreakable, and he was prepared to sacrifice anything in order to protect it and preserve it.

Even though he was aware of the fact that he couldn't survive without her, the worry that he would be found out was something that was always present in the back of his mind. They were under an obligation to maintain secrecy at all costs, which demanded extreme vigilance.

The risk of being caught was a constant reminder of the severe penalty they were subjecting themselves to as a result of their illicit love. But he was confident that so long as they had each other, they would be able to overcome any obstacle.

Chapter 12: The Green-Eyed Monster - Jealousy Rears its Ugly Head

He had never been a jealous person in his life, but now he found that the emotion consumed him completely. Even though he was aware that what they were doing was dangerous, the possibility of him losing her to another person was intolerable to him.

The ugly face of the monster with the green eyes had appeared, and he had no idea how to put it under control. He desired to have her all to himself and did not want anyone else to be able to win her heart.

He was well aware that he was behaving in an irrational manner and that he was unable to control her in every way. However, the fear of being without her was too powerful to be ignored.

He was helpless as the monster with the green eyes continued to consume him, and he had no idea how to stop it. He resented every man who came close to her because he was paranoid that they would take her away from him.

He was aware that he needed to rein in his feelings of resentment in order to trust her and their love for one another. However, the worry that he would be without her proved to be too much, and he found himself succumbing to the green-eyed monster.

The feelings of envy that he had were like a poison that seeped into everything that he did. No matter how hard he tried to get away from it, he was unable to do so.

The monster with the green eyes served as a constant reminder of the price that they had to pay for their illicit love. In order for him to trust her and their love for one another, he had to overcome his tendency toward jealousy.

But the worry that he wouldn't be able to keep her was too much, and as a result, he found himself always on edge and always consumed by jealousy.

The monster with the green eyes was similar to a beast that had taken control of his mind. He was aware that he needed to exercise self-control in order to trust her and their love for one another. However, it was much simpler to say than to actually do.

The feeling of envy that he had was all-encompassing, and he was well aware that he needed to locate a way to put an end to it. He couldn't give it that much power over his life or else he would lose everything that was important to him.

The monster with the green eyes served as a constant reminder of the high cost that they were paying for their illicit love. Otherwise, everything would come to an end if he didn't figure out how to trust her and get control of his jealousy.

The feeling of envy that he had was comparable to a disease, as it permeated every aspect of his life. He was aware that he needed to figure out a way to gain control of it in order to trust her and their love for one another.

The presence of the monster with the green eyes served as a constant warning of the peril they were in. It was imperative that he control his feelings of resentment toward her and have faith in their relationship; otherwise, everything would be lost.

Chapter 13: The Pain of Separation - Longing for What Cannot Be

He had never been in a situation in which he had to endure the anguish of being parted from someone. They had to be cautious in order to conceal the fact that they were having an affair, and this required them to spend time apart.

He grievously missed her, especially the way she smelled and the sensation she gave him when she was in his arms. He yearned to be in her presence, to sense her touch, and to be certain that she was an actual person.

The anguish of being apart from her was as intense as a physical pain in his chest. No matter how hard he tried to get away from it, he was unable to do so.

He was aware that they were putting themselves in harm's way and that their love was perilous. On the other hand, he was conscious of the fact that he was unable to abandon her. The very idea of being without her was too painful to bear.

The anguish of being parted served as a constant reminder of what they were unable to achieve. They were forced to keep their affair a secret, which resulted in them spending the majority of their time apart.

It was her touch, the sound of her voice, and the way that she looked at him that he yearned for the most. However, he was also aware that he was unable to have those things, not without putting everything they had worked so hard for at risk.

The anguish of being parted from her was like a knife thrust into his chest. He desired to be with her, to be able to hold her, and to prevent her from ever leaving his side. However, he was also aware that he needed to exercise caution in order to protect the privacy of their affair.

The anguish of being apart from her was a constant reminder of what they were unable to have together, and he missed her more than words could possibly express. However, he was also aware that he was unable to abandon her, especially given the intensity of the love they shared for one another.

The agony of being parted served as a constant reminder of the severe penalty they were subjecting themselves to as a result of their illicit love. He was well aware of the need for discretion in order to protect the privacy of their affair. However, this did not in any way lessen the intensity of the pain.

He yearned to be with her, to take her into his arms and to keep her in his life forever. However, the anguish of being apart served as a constant reminder of what they were unable to have.

He would never be able to get over the anguish that came with being apart. It was a constant reminder of the illicit love that they had for one another and the terrible price that they had to pay for it. However, he was also aware that he was unable to abandon her, especially given the intensity of the love they shared for one another.

Chapter 14: The Temptation of Confession - Telling the Truth

He had been struggling against the temptation of confession for a considerable amount of time. He was acutely aware that what they were doing was immoral, and the guilt that he felt about it was consuming him.

He desired to make his transgressions known to another person so that he could be released from his sense of responsibility. But he was also aware that it would ruin everything that they had labored for over the years.

The desire to confess was like a burden that was constantly pressing down on his shoulders. No matter how hard he tried to get away from it, he was unable to do so.

He was well aware that he had a responsibility to conceal their affair from their respective families and friends. However, the guilt was too much for him to bear, and he found himself being constantly tempted to reveal the secret to another person.

The allure of confession served as a timely reminder of the severe penalty they were subjecting themselves to as a result of their illicit relationship. He was well aware of the need for discretion in order to protect the privacy of their affair. On the other hand, the guilt was eating him up, and he wasn't sure how much longer he could continue to suppress it.

He desired to make his transgressions known to another person so that he could be released from his sense of responsibility. But he was also aware that it would ruin everything that they had labored for over the years.

The desire to confess was raging within him like a fire that couldn't be extinguished. No matter how hard he tried to get away from it, he was unable to do so.

He was well aware of the need to exercise caution in order to protect their relationship from being discovered. However, the guilt was eating away at him, and he found himself constantly tempted to divulge the information to another person.

The allure of confession served as a constant reminder to them that what they were doing was immoral. However, he was also aware that he was unable to abandon her, especially given the intensity of the love they shared for one another.

He desired to make his transgressions known to another person so that he could be released from his sense of responsibility. But he was also aware that it would ruin everything that they had labored for over the years.

The temptation to confess was building up inside of him like a storm waiting to break. No matter how hard he tried to get away from it, he was unable to do so.

He was well aware of the need to exercise caution in order to protect their relationship from being discovered. However, the guilt was eating him up, and he found that he was constantly tempted to tell someone about what had happened.

The allure of confession served as a timely reminder of the severe penalty they were subjecting themselves to as a result of their illicit relationship. He was well aware of the need for discretion in order to protect the privacy of their affair. Nevertheless, the guilt served as a persistent reminder to them that what they were doing was immoral.

He desired to make his transgressions known to another person so that he could be released from his sense of responsibility. But he was also aware that it would ruin everything that they had labored for over the years.

The allure of confession served as a constant reminder that their love was fraught with peril. However, he was also aware that he was unable to abandon her, especially given the intensity of the love they shared for one another. He would never forget the temptation of confession because it was something that would always serve as a constant reminder of the high price that they were paying for their illicit love.

Chapter 15: The Consequences of Betrayal - Hearts Broken

Before this moment, he had never before had a true comprehension of the repercussions that come along with betrayal. Because he had allowed his feelings for her to consume him, he had been unaware of the effect that their affair was having on those around them.

He had cheated his wife, as well as the rest of his family and his close friends. Because he betrayed their trust in him, the repercussions were extremely negative.

He knew that he could never make up for the harm that he had done to the people whose trust he had betrayed, and their hearts were broken as a result.

The repercussions of his treachery hit him like a tsunami when it all came crashing down on him. No matter how hard he tried to get away from them, he was unable to do so.

Because he was so preoccupied with his feelings for her, he was oblivious to the anguish that he was causing to those who were close to him. Because of his selfish actions, he was now experiencing the consequences of those actions.

The repercussions of their betrayal served as a reminder of the high cost that they were incurring as a result of their illicit love. Because he had allowed himself to become so preoccupied with his attraction to her, he had been unaware of the effect that their affair was having on third parties.

He knew that he could never fully make amends for what he had done because he had broken hearts and ruined lives, and he was okay with that.

The repercussions of his treachery were like a burden from which he could never free himself. He had acted dishonestly toward those who were closest to him, and he was aware that the damage he had done could never be completely undone.

He was forced to deal with the repercussions of his actions and the anguish that he had brought into the world. The fact that he had broken so many people's hearts served as a constant reminder of what he had accomplished, and he was well aware that he would never be able to rectify the situation completely.

The repercussions of their betrayal served as a reminder of the high cost that they were incurring as a result of their illicit love. He was forced to confront the repercussions of his actions and endure the suffering that he had brought into the world.

He had lied to and betrayed the people who were closest to him, and the results were catastrophic. He needed to find a way to make amends for what he had done and then move on with his life. He also needed to find a way to live with what he had done.

The repercussions of his treachery felt like he was carrying a heavy weight on his shoulders. He was responsible for breaking many people's hearts, and he needed to find a way to put things right and make amends.

The repercussions of their betrayal served as a timely reminder that the love they shared was risky. He had to figure out how to move on, how to live with the suffering that he had brought into the world. He would never forget the consequences of the betrayal, which served as a constant reminder of the high price they were paying for their illicit love.

Chapter 16: The Hope of Redemption - Forgiveness and Second Chances

He clung to the possibility of being redeemed despite the overwhelming evidence to the contrary. He was aware that he had erred and that he had caused pain to those who were dearest to him.

But he was also aware that he couldn't let go of hope and that he needed to locate a way to make up for his mistakes and move on with his life.

The possibility of redemption shone like a beacon of light in the gloom. He was helpless to get away from his errors, but he was also aware that he couldn't let them come to define who he was.

He needed to find a way to put things in order, to ask for forgiveness, and to take advantage of second chances.

The possibility of redemption served as a constant reminder that it was never too late to put things right, even in the most dire of circumstances. He was responsible for his actions and had to deal with the consequences of those actions, but he was also aware that he could find a way to move on.

It was necessary for him to seek forgiveness from those he had wronged and to seek them out in order to make amends. The possibility of being forgiven served as a compass, pointing him in the direction of a brighter future.

The concept of redemption served as a constant reminder that we are capable of forgiving others and that second chances do exist. He needed to have faith in himself and his ability to put things in the right direction.

It was necessary for him to devise a strategy that would enable him to regain the confidence and forgiveness of those he had wronged. The possibility of redemption served as a gentle nudge to remind him that it was doable and that he could locate some way to make amends for his actions.

A glimmer of light shone through the murky clouds whenever there was the possibility of redemption. It was necessary for him to have faith that he could put things in order and discover a solution so that he could move on.

In order to gain the forgiveness of those he had wronged and the confidence they had in him, he had to seek them out and make amends. The belief that one could be saved served as a constant reminder that it was never too late to begin again.

A reminder that their love was something that was worth fighting for was provided by the possibility of redemption. It was imperative that he discover a means whereby he could put things right and win the forgiveness of those whom he had wronged.

In order to trust that he could put things in order, he needed to have faith in the transformative potential of second chances. The possibility of redemption served as a reminder that it was not only doable, but also that he could locate a way to move on with his life and build a better future for himself.

The possibility of redemption served as a soothing balm to his broken spirit. In order for him to have faith that he could put things back in order, he needed to look for forgiveness and opportunities for do-overs.

The possibility of redemption served as a reminder that the two of them had a love that was worth fighting for and that he needed to keep doing so. Even in the face of betrayal, the possibility of redemption served as a constant reminder to him that forgiveness and second chances were still open to him. This was something that he would never forget.

Chapter 17: The Desire for Normalcy - Can Love Survive in the Light?

Since the beginning, he had been nursing a longing for things to return to their usual state, which was normalcy. He yearned for the day when he could declare his love for her without the burden of hiding their relationship from others.

But he was also aware that the two of them were putting themselves in harm's way by falling in love, and that coming clean could ruin everything they had worked for.

The yearning for normalcy served as a compass, pointing him in the direction of a time and place in the future where their love could flourish in the open.

He yearned for the day when he could confidently take her out on dates and hold her hand in public without the risk of being discovered. He dreamed of a future with her, one in which they would be able to share their lives with his friends and family.

But he was also aware that the two of them were not supposed to be together, and that if the truth were revealed, it could have devastating effects.

The yearning for normalcy served as a constant reminder of what they were unable to achieve. They were obligated to conceal their affair from their families and friends in order to do what was best.

But he also knew that he couldn't let go of hope, that there had to be a way for their love to work even in the light, and that he couldn't give up on finding a solution.

The yearning for normalcy was similar to a dream that he was unable to fully comprehend. He was aware that it would require a significant amount of effort on his part, but he was also aware that the outcome would be worthwhile.

He desired to be able to spend the rest of his life with her and to not be forced to keep their love a secret from the world.

That their love was something that was worth fighting for and that they needed to find a way to make it work in the light was brought home to them by their yearning for normalcy.

He was well aware that it would not be simple and that there would be difficulties to overcome along the way. But he was also aware that they needed to make an effort because their love was too powerful to be kept a secret any longer.

The need for things to return to their usual state was like a fire raging within him. He had to figure out a way to make their relationship work so that they wouldn't have to keep their relationship a secret.

He was aware that they would need to take their time and be cautious throughout the process. But he also knew that they were capable of achieving their goal, and that their love was powerful enough to endure even when exposed to daylight.

The need for things to be as they always were served as a timely reminder that they could not keep their affair a secret indefinitely. They needed to figure out how to make their love work so that they wouldn't have to keep it a secret.

He was aware that doing so would involve some danger, but he also understood that it was an opportunity that should not be passed up. The aspiration for normalcy served as a beacon, pointing them in the direction of a time and place in the future where their love could be expressed openly.

The yearning for things to return to their usual course was something he would never forget. It served as a timely reminder that their love was something worth fighting for, and that they needed to figure out how to make it work in the open.

Chapter 18: The Impending Threat - Danger Looms on the Horizon

The impending danger was something that he had been fearing ever since it was first brought to his attention. He was well aware that their love was risky and that they were putting themselves in harm's way whenever they were together.

However, the threat was now more tangible than ever before. Someone else was aware of their affair, someone who had the ability to blow the whistle on them and ruin everything they had worked for up to that point.

The impending danger was comparable to a menacing cloud that was gathering on the horizon. No matter how hard he tried to get away from it, he was unable to do so.

He was well aware that they needed to tread carefully so as not to reveal any hints about the affair they were having. However, the danger was always present, waiting in the shadows to strike.

The looming danger served as a timely reminder of the peril they were putting themselves in and the severe penalty they were subjecting themselves to as a result of their illicit relationship.

He needed to devise a plan to shield her from danger and keep her out of harm's way. The impending danger served as a kind of warning, informing him that they were getting shorter and shorter on time.

In order to safeguard the privacy of their relationship, he had to exercise extreme caution. But the danger was always present, serving as a constant reminder of what they were putting themselves at risk for.

The impending danger was comparable to a sword that was poised to cut them down at any moment. He had to come up with a strategy that would safeguard their love and prevent it from being shattered by those who wanted to see it broken up.

He was well aware of the need for discretion in order to protect the privacy of their affair. However, the looming danger was always present, serving as a constant reminder of the peril they faced.

The impending danger was comparable to a storm that was brewing in the distance. He had to come up with a strategy to get through it in order to keep their love from being torn apart by the storm.

He could not afford to relax his vigilance or let his guard down. The looming danger was always there, just sitting around and waiting for the right opportunity to strike.

The looming danger served as a timely reminder that their love was perilous and that they ran the risk of being hurt whenever they were in each other's company. However, he was also aware that he was unable to abandon her, especially given the intensity of the love they shared for one another.

In order to conceal the nature of their relationship and ensure her safety, he was going to have to devise a plan. The impending danger served as a wake-up call, alerting him to the fact that he needed to be prepared to fight for their love.

The looming danger was something that he would never let himself forget. It served as a reminder that their love was something worth fighting for, and that they needed to find a way to shield it from those who would take pleasure in seeing it broken apart.

Chapter 19: The Sacrifice of Self - Choosing Love over All Else

He had never in his wildest dreams anticipated being put in a position where he would have to make such a personal sacrifice. He had a long-standing commitment to the principle of putting his own requirements first and acting in a manner that was in his own self-interest.

But now he was in a position where he had to make a decision. He had the option of choosing his own happiness, or he could select the option of being with the woman he loved.

The offer of self-sacrifice was analogous to a fork in the road, and it compelled him to make a choice that would alter the trajectory of the rest of his life.

He was well aware that if he made the decision to be with her, it would require him to forgo every other aspect of his life. His decision would have repercussions not only for him but also for his friends and family as well.

However, he was also aware that he was unable to abandon her, especially given the intensity of the love they shared for one another.

The self-sacrifice served as a poignant reminder that, in certain circumstances, love compels us to forego everything else. To put love ahead of everything else in his life, he needed to be willing to make the ultimate sacrifice.

To be able to choose a life with her rather than one filled with comfort and safety, he needed to be willing to put everything on the line for her.

The self-sacrifice served as a kind of litmus test for his devotion. In order for him to be with her, he had to be prepared to forgo all other aspects of his life.

He was aware that the path ahead would be difficult and that there would be obstacles to overcome along the way. On the other hand, he was aware of the fact that he was unable to picture his life after she had left it.

The giving up of oneself as a sacrifice was a powerful reminder that love is something that is worth fighting for. To put love ahead of everything else in his life, he needed to be willing to make the ultimate sacrifice.

He had to be willing to put her first, to choose a life with her even if it meant sacrificing everything else in order to do so, and to choose a life with her.

The self-sacrifice was comparable to taking a leap of faith. He needed to have faith that the strength of his feelings for her would be sufficient, and that they would find a way to make their relationship work no matter what.

To put love ahead of everything else in his life, he needed to be willing to make the ultimate sacrifice. It was a reminder that their love was worth fighting for, and that he had to be willing to give up everything else in order to be with her. His sacrifice of himself served as this reminder.

The self-sacrifice was an experience that he would never forget in his life. It served as a reminder that love often demanded that we put everything else on the line for the people we cared about, and that we had to be willing to do whatever it took to make that happen.

Chapter 20: The Power of Trust - Building a Foundation for Love

He had never before gained a proper appreciation for the power that came with trusting others, but that had changed now. He had the preconceived notion that trust was something that could be easily gained and just as easily lost.

But now he understood that trust was the cornerstone upon which their love was built. If they didn't trust each other, their relationship would never last.

The strength of their relationship was like a bridge between them, providing a deeper level of connection between them both. Even when things got difficult, he had to be willing to trust her and believe in her. He had to have faith in her.

In order to be vulnerable and open with her, he needed to be willing to share his deepest, darkest secrets with her. The strength of trust served as a reminder that in order to love someone else, we needed to be willing to take chances and trust others despite the difficulty of the situation.

The strength of their relationship was comparable to a blazing fire, and it burned brightly between them. He had to tend to it in order to make certain that it would never die out.

He had to be willing to trust her even when he didn't fully understand her, and he had to be willing to believe in her even when he was full of doubts about their relationship.

The strength of trust served as a reminder that love demanded that we be willing to let go of our anxieties and skepticisms, to make a leap of faith, and to put our faith and trust in the people we loved.

The strength of trust was comparable to that of a foundation; it was solid and reliable. In order to construct a life with her that was founded on trust and love, he needed to be willing to build on what they had.

In order for them to make progress together toward a shared objective, it was necessary for him to be open about sharing his hopes and ambitions with her. The strength of their trust served as a constant reminder that the love they shared was something that was worth fighting for and that he needed to be willing to put in the effort to ensure that it would last.

The healing balm that trust could be was to his very being. Even though it was difficult, he needed to have faith in her and trust in her.

Because he wanted to believe that she had his best interests at heart, he needed to be willing to forgive her when she made mistakes. The strength of their trust served as a reminder that the effort required to maintain their love was well worth it and that he needed to be willing to put in the effort if he wanted it to last.

He was determined to never lose sight of the significance of trust in his life. It served as a reminder that love required us to be willing to put ourselves in potentially dangerous situations, to be honest and open with the people we loved, and to take risks.

Even when things got difficult, he had to be willing to trust her and believe in her. He had to have faith in her. They were directed toward a future filled with love and happiness by the strength of trust, which acted as a compass or a lighthouse for them.

Chapter 21: The Rekindling of Passion - Rediscovering Each Other

Since the beginning, all he wanted was for the flame of passion that once burned between them to be reignited once more. He had no doubt that their love was intense and passionate from the beginning, but in recent months, he had the impression that something was lacking.

Now, however, he had the impression that they were getting to know one another better, as though the ardor that once existed between them had been reignited.

The rekindling of their passion served as a reminder that their love was something that was worth fighting for and was like a second chance.

He had the impression that they were rediscovering each other and that they were going through the process of falling in love all over again. The rekindling of their passion served as a timely reminder that there was more to their love than merely a physical attraction; rather, there was something more substantial that bound them together.

He had the impression that they were connecting on a more profound level, as though they were rediscovering the reasons why they had initially fallen in love with one another.

The reawakening of his passion served as kindling that stoked an existing blaze within him. In order for them to rediscover one another and start falling in love all over again, he needed to be willing to let go of the past and concentrate on the here and now.

In order to be honest and open with her, he needed to be willing to expose himself to risk and be vulnerable. The rekindling of their passion served as a reminder that the love they shared was worth the work and that he needed to be willing to put in the effort to ensure that it would continue.

The process of reigniting a dormant passion was analogous to going on an adventure to discover oneself. In order to have an open and honest conversation with her, he needed to be willing to investigate his own wants and requirements.

In order for him to have faith in the strength of their love, he needed to be willing to let go of his worries and doubts. The reawakening of their passion served as a timely reminder that their love was something that was worth fighting for and that he needed to be willing to take chances in order to make it work.

The reigniting of passion was like taking a deep calming breath of new air. He had the impression that they were getting to know one another better, almost as if they were falling in love all over again.

It was necessary for him to have the willingness to put in the work, patience, and understanding. The rekindling of their passion served as a reminder that love was not only about the good times that they shared together, but also about the difficulties that they overcame as a unit.

The reigniting of a dormant passion felt like the start of something brand new. In order for them to rediscover one another and start falling in love all over again, he needed to be willing to let go of the past and concentrate on the here and now.

In order to be honest and open with her, he needed to be willing to expose himself to risk and be vulnerable. The rekindling of their passion served as a reminder that the love they shared was worth the work and that he needed to be willing to put in the effort to ensure that it would continue.

The reigniting of passion was an experience that he would never let slip from his mind. It served as a reminder that their love was worth fighting for, and that in order to keep the fire of their love burning brightly, he needed to be willing to take risks and make sacrifices.

Chapter 22: The Strength of Unity - Facing Adversity Together

In spite of the fact that he had always been aware that the power of unity was significant, it wasn't until now that he realized how vitally important it was to their connection.

They had encountered an incredible number of difficulties and challenges, but they had always been able to triumph over them because they were united and faced adversity together.

They were shielded from the dangers of the outside world by the fortitude that came from their unity. He was aware of the fact that he could depend on her and that she would never abandon him despite the circumstances.

He had the impression that they were members of the same group pursuing the same objective. They were reminded by the power of unity that they were much more powerful as a group than they were individually.

He was aware that they needed to be willing to make concessions, as well as communicate with each other in an open and forthright manner. The power of cohesiveness served as a timely reminder that their love was something worth fighting for and that they needed to cooperate in order to triumph over any challenges that stood in their way.

They were held together by an unbreakable and powerful bond that was the power of their unity. It seemed to him that they were always on the same page, as though each of them knew exactly what the other was considering at any given moment.

It was necessary for him to demonstrate an openness to her point of view as well as respect for her opinions and convictions. That their love was more than just a physical attraction and that it was a profound and significant connection between them was brought home to them by the fact that their unity was so strong.

He had the impression that they were taking on the entire world together, and that so long as they remained united, nothing could stop them from achieving their goals. The power of their combined efforts served as a timely reminder that they needed to be willing to put in the effort to maintain a healthy relationship with one another.

The power that came from working together shone like a beacon in the gloom. He had the impression that they were capable of overcoming any challenge that came their way because they were working together.

In order to give her the space she required at the times when she required it, he needed to be willing to show patience and understanding. The power of unity served as a timely reminder that their love was worth the effort, and that they needed to cooperate in order to triumph over any obstacles that stood in their way.

A shining example of hope was provided by the power of unity. He had the impression that they were taking on the entire world together, and that so long as they remained united, they could triumph over anything.

In order to put her needs ahead of his own and collaborate toward achieving a common objective, he had to be willing to let go of his own wants and needs. That their love was more than just a physical attraction and that it was a profound and significant connection between them was brought home to them by the fact that their unity was so strong.

He would never forget the power that came from having everyone pull together. It served as a reminder that their love was something worth fighting for, that they needed to be willing to put in the effort together and face any challenges as a unified front.

Chapter 23: The Unveiling of Truth - Secrets Revealed

The revelation of the truth was something that he had always been afraid of, but now he understood that it was essential for their relationship to move forward in order to accomplish this.

Because they were concerned about the other person's reaction, they had been keeping secrets from one another. However, at this point, they needed to be willing to expose the truth in order to face the repercussions as a group.

The revelation of the truth was similar to having a burden removed from his shoulders. For far too long, he had been forced to bear the burden of his secrets, and now he understood that he had no choice but to be truthful with her.

In order to take responsibility for his errors and be willing to face the consequences of his actions, he needed to be willing to face the consequences of his actions. The revelation of the truth served as a timely reminder that their love was something that was worth fighting for, and that he needed to be willing to put in the effort necessary to make things right.

The exposure of the lie served as something akin to a turning point in their relationship. They needed to be willing to trust one another, which required them to be vulnerable and honest about how they felt.

He had the impression that they were getting to know one another on a more profound level, and that their relationship was developing into something that was deeper and had greater significance.

The revelation of the truth served as a timely reminder that the two of them shared something that went far beyond a simple physical attraction; rather, it was a profound and significant bond between them.

In order to comprehend her standpoint, he needed to be willing to pay attention to what she had to say. The revelation of the truth served as a timely reminder that they needed to be open to collaboration and compromise in order to surmount any challenges that stood in their way.

The exposure of the truth was akin to the introduction of a new element. He had the impression that they were entering a new era in their relationship, one that was founded on openness and confidence.

It was necessary for him to be willing to apologize for his errors, take responsibility for them, and make amends. The revelation of the truth served as a timely reminder that their love was something that was worth fighting for, and that he needed to be willing to put in the effort necessary to make things right.

The exposure of the truth was similar to a test of their love for one another. It was necessary for him to exhibit understanding and compassion, as well as a willingness to forgive her for the errors she had committed.

He had the impression that they were closer than they had ever been, and that their love had grown stronger as a result of the truth that they had uncovered. The revelation of the truth served as a timely reminder that their love was something that was worth fighting for, and that they needed to be willing to put in the effort necessary to ensure that it would endure.

The revelation of the truth was an experience that he would never let pass from his mind. It served as a timely reminder that their love was something worth fighting for, and that in order to move forward, they needed to be willing to be honest and vulnerable with each other.

Chapter 24: The Triumph of Love - Overcoming All Odds

He had never before gained a proper appreciation for the triumph of love, but that was about to change. They had encountered a great number of difficulties and roadblocks, but their love had prevailed over all of the odds.

He had the impression that they were a unit that was taking on the world together. The fact that love ultimately prevailed served as a timely reminder that their love was capable of overcoming any challenge that was thrown their way.

To be her pillar of support and source of fortitude in a time of greatest need, he needed to be willing to fight for her. The victory of love served as a timely reminder that they were more powerful as a unit than they were as individuals.

He had the impression that they were traveling through life together, experiencing all of its highs and lows as a team. The victory of love served as a timely reminder that they needed to be prepared to put in the effort necessary for their relationship to endure.

In order to have an honest and open dialogue with her, he needed to demonstrate a willingness to be patient and understanding with her. The realization that their love was something worth fighting for and that they needed to work together in order to overcome any challenges that stood in their way was brought home to them by the victory of love.

The victory of love served as a symbol of hope, lighting the way toward a more promising future. He had the impression that their love had prevailed over so many obstacles that it had become even more powerful as a result of them.

In order to put her needs ahead of his own and collaborate toward achieving a common objective, he had to be willing to let go of his own wants and needs. The victory of love served as a reminder that their love consisted of more than merely a physical attraction between them; rather, it was a profound and significant bond between the two of them.

The victory of love was comparable to a victory, a celebration of all that they had triumphed over. He had the impression that they were more powerful than they had ever been, and that their love had triumphed over everything.

It was necessary for him to demonstrate an openness to her point of view as well as respect for her opinions and convictions. The realization that their love was something worth fighting for and that they needed to work together in order to overcome any obstacles that they encountered was brought home to them by the victory of love.

The triumph of love served as a reminder that if they were willing to put in the effort, they could achieve anything they set their minds to. He had the impression that as long as they were committed to their love for one another and stayed together, nothing could stop them from achieving their goals.

In order to be honest and open with her, he needed to be willing to expose himself to risk and be vulnerable. The realization that their love was worth the effort and that they needed to be willing to put in the work to make it last was brought on by the success of love.

The victory of love was an experience that he would never let himself forget. It served as a reminder that their love was something that was worth fighting for, and that they needed to be willing to face any challenges that came their way, as long as they were together and unified in their love for each other.

Chapter 25: The Price of Happiness - Is It Worth It?

He had never before given much thought to the cost of happiness; however, at this point in time, he did so. He had always held the conviction that one's level of contentment was the single most important factor in one's life and that everything else paled in comparison to this.

On the other hand, now that he had arrived at this point, he understood that happiness did not come without its fair share of difficulties and concessions.

He was of the opinion that in order for them to be happy, they needed to be willing to face challenging decisions and give up certain things. A reminder that their love was something that was worth fighting for and that they needed to be willing to make sacrifices in order to make it work was the "price of happiness."

In order for him to find the happiness that he was searching for, he had to be willing to challenge himself and move outside of his comfort zone. That their love was worth the effort and that he needed to be willing to put in the work to make it last was a lesson that he learned from the book "The Price of Happiness."

The price of happiness served as a test of the couple's love for one another. It was necessary for him to have the flexibility to make concessions and pay attention to her wants and requirements.

He was of the opinion that in order for them to find genuine contentment, they needed to be willing to cooperate and communicate in an open and sincere manner. The realization that happiness comes at a cost served as a timely reminder that their love could overcome any challenge that was thrown their way.

In order for him to have faith in the strength of their love, he needed to be willing to let go of his worries and doubts. A reminder that their love was something that was worth fighting for and that he needed to be willing to take risks in order to make it work was the "price of happiness."

The pursuit of happiness was analogous to going on a trip, complete with numerous turns and curves. He had the impression that they were moving in the direction of something more significant, toward a future that was full of love and happiness.

He had to be willing to take responsibility for his actions and accept both the positive and negative outcomes of his decisions. That their love was something that was worth fighting for and that he needed to be willing to put in the effort to make it last was brought home to him by the realization that happiness comes at a cost.

The difficulty of achieving happiness served as a stark illustration of the fact that nothing of value ever comes without effort. He believed that in order for them to be happy, they needed to be willing to put in the effort to achieve their goals and work for what they wanted.

To be able to fully appreciate the joy that they shared together and appreciate the present moment, he needed to be willing to let go of the past and concentrate on the here and now. That their love was something that was worth fighting for and that he needed to be willing to put in the effort to make it last was brought home to him by the realization that happiness comes at a cost.

He would never, ever forget the cost of happiness. It was something he would always value. It served as a reminder that their love was something worth fighting for, and that in order for them to find true happiness together, they needed to be willing to make sacrifices and take risks.

Chapter 26: The Bittersweet Goodbye - Love Never Dies

The painful parting was something that he had always dreaded, but now that he had experienced it, he understood that it was an inevitable part of life.

Their love had been so robust and potent, but it was time for them to part ways now. Even though he knew that their love would last forever, it was still difficult for him to let go of it. This made the situation bittersweet.

He was of the opinion that they needed to be willing to value the time they spent together and strive to make the most of the remaining opportunities they had. That their love was something that was worth fighting for and that they needed to be willing to make the most of every moment was brought home to them by the bittersweet farewell.

In order for him to have faith in the strength of their love, he needed to be willing to let go of his worries and doubts. The painful parting served as a reminder that their love consisted of more than just a physical attraction between the two of them; rather, it was a profound and significant bond between the two of them.

The painful parting was almost like a party to celebrate their love for one another. He had the impression that they had triumphed over a great deal of adversity and struggle together, and that they had become much more successful as a result.

In order to properly grieve their loss, he needed to be willing to suffer through the anguish of parting ways with them. It was a bittersweet farewell, but it served as a reminder that their love was something worth fighting for, and that he needed to be willing to feel the pain in order to move on.

The painful experience of saying goodbye served as a powerful reminder that their love would last forever. He had the impression that the love they shared would outlast them both and continue to exist even after they were gone.

It was necessary for him to be ready to keep the memories they had shared with one another, to treasure them for the rest of his life. The sour and sweet farewell served as a reminder that their love was something worth fighting for, and that he needed to be willing to keep the memory of their love alive in his heart.

The sour and sweet farewell served as a poignant reminder that nothing lasts for all of time. In order to maximize the potential of the time they had together, he believed that they needed to be open to the idea that everything in life is temporary.

To honor their love and everything that they had accomplished together, he needed to be willing to bid farewell with affection and gratitude. This was a requirement. It was a bittersweet farewell, but it served as a reminder that their love was worth fighting for, and that in order for him to move on, he had to be willing to let go.

The painfully emotional farewell was an experience that he would never forget. It served as a constant reminder that their love was unending and that it would continue on after both of them had passed away. It served as a gentle yet powerful reminder that their love was something worth fighting for, that it was a profound and significant connection that would never really be severed.

Also by IVY BLAIR

Breathless Desire: A Tale of Passion and Obsession
The Perfect Match: A Love Story Written in the Stars
The Passionate Pursuit: A Tale of Forbidden Love and Unbridled
Desire

About the Publisher

Accepting manuscripts in the most categories. We love to help people get their words available to the world.

Revival Waves of Glory focus is to provide more options to be published. We do traditional paperbacks, hardcovers, audio books and ebooks all over the world. A traditional royalty-based publisher that offers self-publishing options, Revival Waves provides a very author friendly and transparent publishing process, with President Bill Vincent involved in the full process of your book. Send us your manuscript and we will contact you as soon as possible.

Contact: Bill Vincent at rwgpublishing@yahoo.com

Printed in May 2023
by Rotomail Italia S.p.A., Vignate (MI) - Italy